To Celia, who climbed the mountain with me - *MD*

First published in Great Britain in 2000 by Bloomsbury Publishing Plc
38 Soho Square, London W1V 5DF

Text copyright © Malachy Doyle 2000
Illustrations copyright © Giles Greenfield 2000
The moral right of the author and illustrator has been asserted

A CIP catalogue record for this book is available from the British Library
ISBN 0 7475 4770 X

Designed by Dawn Apperley

Printed and bound by South China Printing Co

1 3 5 7 9 10 8 6 4 2

Owen and the Mountain

Malachy Doyle
and Giles Greenfield

BLOOMSBURY
CHILDREN'S
BOOKS

Owen went to stay with his grandad.
Grandad lived on his own, in a cottage
at the foot of a mountain. He had no
television. He had no car. It was a
long time since he'd had a child to stay.

'What would you like to do, Owen?' asked Grandad.

Owen looked out of the window. All he could see was the great mountain, rising to the sky.

'I suppose we could play a game,' said Grandad, trying to think of one.

'I don't want to play a game,' said Owen, 'I want to go up there, to the top of the mountain.'

Grandad said nothing for a long time.

'I'm sorry, Owen,' he sighed, 'you're too young to walk to the top of the mountain. And I'm too old.'

Later, Grandad went to Owen's room to say goodnight. He found him sitting by the window.

'Grandad,' said Owen, 'the sheep can climb the mountain, even the old ones. Please can we try?'

Grandad sat next to him, and they were quiet.

'All right, Owen,' he said, at last. 'If it's fine tomorrow, we'll try to climb the mountain.'

Early the next morning Owen ran along the path. He stopped at the edge of the woods.

'It's dark in there, Grandad,' he said. 'I don't like it.'

'It's all right, Owen,' said Grandad, coming close. 'Take my hand. Can you hear the birds?' he whispered, as they entered the woods.

Owen listened. He heard the birds singing in the trees. They walked a little further.

'Can you hear the wind?' asked Grandad.

Owen listened, and heard the wind sighing in the leaves.

'I like the woods, Grandad,' said Owen, as they came out into the daylight. 'I like the woods when I'm with you.'

The path up the mountain was steep and stony. It was easier for Grandad, with his grown-up legs, but it was hard for little Owen.

'I'm tired, Grandad,' he said, as they came to the bubbling stream. 'Can we stop?'

'Of course we can, Owen,' said Grandad. 'We can stop as often as you like.'

Grandad showed Owen how to cup his hands to drink the fresh clear water, and they rested.

'The path's not so steep now, Owen,' said Grandad. 'Would you like to ride on my shoulders?'

'Oh yes, Grandad!' said Owen.

So Grandad lifted him up and bounced him along, high in the air.

'I like it here, Grandad,' said Owen. 'I like it in the mountains with you.

Soon they came to a beautiful lake. Owen laughed, throwing pebbles into the shining water. He laughed some more, as Grandad showed him how to choose smooth, flat stones, and bounce them across the lake.

'Isn't it wonderful, Owen?' said Grandad, stretching out on the grassy bank. 'I could stay here all day.'

But Owen didn't want to stay. He wanted to get to the top of the mountain.

'Come on, Grandad!' he called, running off up the path.

Slowly Grandad got to his feet.

'Wait for me, Owen,' he cried. 'Don't go on your own!'

Owen clambered up the steep slope. When he got to the narrow ridge, it was cold, so cold, and the wind took his breath away.
Owen looked all around, and he was frightened. He looked down and saw Grandad, trudging up behind him, and he was glad.

'Grandad!' he cried, shivering. 'I was scared.'
'It's all right, Owen,' said Grandad, holding him tightly. 'You're safe now.'
'I'm sorry I ran off, Grandad,' said Owen. 'I want to be with you now.'

'And I want to be with you, Owen,' said Grandad. 'Here, put on my jumper. You're freezing!'

He took off his big woolly jumper and put it over Owen. It reached down to Owen's knees, and they both laughed.

At last, together, they reached the summit of the great mountain. Owen looked down and he could see the lake, the woods, and even Grandad's cottage, tiny in the distance. He looked up, and there was nothing but sky.

'We're on top of the world, aren't we, Grandad?' he whispered.
'We are, Owen,' said Grandad, putting his arm around him.
Owen snuggled in close, and they were quiet.

The way down was hard for them both, and they had to stop many times, to rest their weary legs.

'My knees are like jelly,' said Owen, catching hold of Grandad.

'So are mine, Owen,' said Grandad, steadying him. 'But if we take it slowly, we'll be fine.'

As the long hard day turned to evening,
they arrived back at the cottage.

Grandad warmed up some soup, and then Owen squashed up beside him in the big cosy armchair.

'I'm glad we climbed the mountain, Grandad,' he said sleepily. 'I'm glad I came to stay.'

'So am I, Owen,' said Grandad, smiling. 'So am I.'